W9-CCM-863

Emily Jenkins Pictures by **Sergio Ruzzier**

Love You When You Whine

Frances Foster Books • Farrar, Straus and Giroux • New York

Love you when you whine.

Love you when you interrupt.

Love you when you don't say "please."

Love you when you pour cereal on the floor.

And when you ask for every toy in the whole store,
one after the other.

Love you when you track in mud.

Love you when you paint the walls . . .

and the dog.

Love you when you won't eat dinner
and then try to get dessert.

And chew with your mouth open.

And throw up on my good wool coat.

Love you when you *scream* "Lollipop lollipop lollipop"
for forty-five minutes on line at the bank.

And when you hide my keys.

And put your crayons in the dryer.

And won't get dressed.

Love you when you mess with my checkbook.

Love you when you unfold all the laundry
I just folded.

Love you when you spread jam on my computer.

Love you, yes, when you are way too loud.

And when you splash me with bathwater.

And pull on my hair.

Love you when you say "Carry me, carry me"
and I am already carrying two bags of groceries
and a backpack full of library books.

Love you when you irritate me.

Love you when you will not share.

Love you when you hit someone.

Love you when you have a tantrum.

Love you, even when you say that
you don't love me.

Love you, always.

Yes, I do.

For Ivy, again and always. And with gratitude for the inspiration.

—E.J.

For Amanda B. and Emily A.

—S.R.

Distributed in Canada by Douglas & McIntyre Ltd.
Color separations by Chroma Graphics PTE Ltd.
Printed and bound in the United States of America by Worzalla
Designed by Barbara Grzeslo
First edition, 2006
1 3 5 7 9 10 8 6 4 2

www.fsgkidsbooks.com

Library of Congress Cataloging-in-Publication Data
Jenkins, Emily, date.
Love you when you whine / Emily Jenkins ; pictures by Sergio Ruzzier.— 1st ed.
p. cm.
Summary: Even while her toddler whines, paints the walls, has tantrums, and otherwise misbehaves, a mother assures her of her love.
ISBN-13: 978-0-374-34652-2
ISBN-10: 0-374-34652-6
[1. Mother and child—Fiction. 2. Love—Fiction.] I. Ruzzier, Sergio, ill. II. Title.

PZ7.J4134Lov 2006
[E]—dc22

2005040122